To Stand Under A Yellow Tree, Imagining

Renie Garlick

This is like no book you have ever read.
Let it be itself in your hands.

I wish to thank first and foremost the mudpeople. It is my greatest joy and highest good to be their faithful servant.

My most profound appreciation to my husband for his generosity and support for this project and all my dreams. Also, to all the members of CrowKula who continually inspire me by their openness to the story, I am grateful. And there are others, especially those early readers whose enthusiastic response went a long way towards making my path clear.

These gifts of such sincere sweetness are deeply touching and cherished. You have all lent your hands to the creation of this offering. Thank you.

preamble

You may remember perhaps,
and already know,
that these words:
"To stand under a yellow tree, imagining"
are themselves a story,
complete and unabridged.
That these words,
this story
is the most beloved
and most honored
of all the stories
of the mudpeople.
And this says much
as the mudpeople are known for the reverence
    they have for stories.
They hold a good story in high esteem
as they would hold a member of their people
who worked healing,
or one who walked the Great Path,

as it is called.
They love stories
the way they love people.
I have learned this much at least from them.
Or, it seems, I have come
to remember this of myself from
my time with them.

In their tradition,
this story
"To stand under a yellow tree, imagining,"
opens the high festivals,
those grand days of bright, continuous story-
    making-story-telling that mark the seasons.
It is meant
to set
before the storytellers and audience alike,
the heights
to which they both ascend in tale-making.
Among the mudpeople
I could find none
who would claim its authoring.
All own it
as a gift of language.
Thus, it has the quality of blessing about it.
Thus, I offer it also as a prayer,
in hope that my tale will have some measure of
    its beauty and sanctity.

Further, I pray
that this offering of mine which follows
be acceptable to the mudpeople.

And do them honor.
Though, as it goes
and must be with language,
it is only a handful of water.

   *Latida.**

* expression meaning "go well"; believed to be derived from
the action or movement of a gate swinging open; possibly the
opening of the *Falling Gate* through which all must pass to
find their path.

The mudpeople come to me
like an alphabet.

They stand along the far edge of my
neighbor's farming field,
among the trees and the night,
and there is a mist low to the ground.
An almost-full moon
heavy with snow
fills bare branches,
lights their bodies and limbs,
their russet baskets and the poles they carry with them,
and traces their shapes against the dark dense
wood like letters in reverse type.

And because I want to learn this language,
I set down
all of my burdens and go on with them.

That is how it was for me. That is how I
began my days among the mudpeople.

But those days are no more
and I no longer pass along the windle paths with them.
And so, must content myself to sit here for
awhile and tell you of them,
their ways and gentle happinesses.
Be sure: it is not for your sake, or for your
entertainment of this evening, that this is done.

I speak to shape for myself some semblance
    of them again
to carry with me
now that I am with them no more.
I ask that you allow me this much.
We may each find some
of our burden
lessened by such practice.

    In its course,
I promise to show you
how the mudpeople live among us,
side by side our own homes and houses.
How they bring us gifts
and fill out our world with unmarked abundance.
I will tell you of days and nights running with them,
    young and old,
through meadow fields
and riverbeds in cool piney woods,
out to oceans roaring
and across prairie hills.
Season upon season of wisdom
and freedom
and happy mysteries.

    These are only fragments
but are worth many years of such nights as this
    I spend with you,
and so,
I will begin.

The mudpeople come to me like an alphabet.
And because I want to learn their language,
   I go on with them.

   I step into woods full.
Well over one hundred of them,
moving in unison,
towards the west,
towards the moon,
a writhing shape of moonlight itself.
Each step takes me further from my bed and
   my life. And I run.

   The trees,
bare and frosted with low solstice light,
turn to me and bend into my path,
twirl and revolve as I pass by
like dancers moving on to another partner.
I say my "Farewell!"
to my familiars,
to my neighbors,
even to the one I love as myself,
leaving them each and all behind as I run on.

   We gather and run on.
Passing through
and up a few doors from what has just been my home,
someone drags garbage to the curb.

I, full with free breathing,
am so close,
close enough to tip the lid off the can.
It comes down with a sodden thud
and then the road hums with our tread and
    low laughter.
He curses
and slumps over to gather it up.
He hasn't recognized me
and does not acknowledge our presence.
I know now that he has not seen us at all.
The mudpeople have taken on the cloak of the night.
And since I have come to travel with them,
I, too, am covered by its mantle.

    In our first hours, they speak an unending tome
low, soft and open as we run.
It seems filled
with my name
and the names of things familiar and once dear to me.
It seems filled with laughing.
And I run on
with the rhythm of its drum in my body.

    We race on.
At times with one
then another
through trees
and the roots of trees,
all along the edges of pastures,
to tumble down hillsides together.
We run with the deer and keep the moon before us.

We stop
to watch a hawk hunt and feed,
and then run on
west again.
I run
as if in a dream,
a full free flight through elemental terrain,
the patterns of light and shadow,
the quick rustle of my companions' breath and limbs,
all push at me to run on.

Does the point of the arrow ask "where?"

We run for hours,
long after daybreak,
silent between ourselves
except for their prayer of welcome
which hangs in the air
long after its praying.
And I would run on for many hours more
but for the gentle hand
placed on my forearm at midmorning
calling me to come to rest.
I feel only happiness
and myself complete.
I smell the scent of pine.
Then I sleep
even before I hit the ground
that has been prepared to accept my sleep.

I awake
and there is a new world peopled
      by graceful creatures
tall and lithe like elegant calligraphy.
With the mudpeople,
or "genG" as they are more properly called,
the average adult stands somewhere near 7 feet.
They are all,
old and young alike,
lean
and long-legged
with large narrowed heads.
And though it takes some getting used to,
I grow to prefer this silhouette
to that of those
like myself, "crows"
as they call us,
shorter
and squat
who have come to travel with them.

      The genG are an ancient nomadic people.
Reclusive and primitive,
they live off the land
and close to nature.
They walk the earth
and are defined by it
for it is this that gives them their name.
"genG",
as they say,

"is the sound of the footfall upon the path."
And for the genG,
while walking is the syntax of their being,
their one meaning
and true purpose
is the story and its telling.
It is to this that they devote themselves and
        all the skill of their manufacture.

        It is the mudpeople who are to be credited
with the creation of alphabet
and the myriad languages spoken and read
throughout the world
from the earliest of times.
They created all the forms
and all the letters
of all the languages modern and ancient,
runes illegible and full of promise,
even the memories
of whisperings
of long lost irrecoverable texts. And more.

        They tell stories in English, in Arabic, and
        in Russian to be sure,
but there is more.
They will write with trees
and the branches of trees,
with cows along rolling pastures and with fireworks.
They make poetry
from their own bodies and limbs.
The mudpeople walk the earth,
on every continent and across vast oceans,

writing in new tongues
and shaped silences,
arranging from
even the shadows themselves
logos.

     Mudpeople write stories in grasses on hillsides
and along country roads.
Winds finger through the text and
the fronds turn and
speak the words written there.
Mostly they say
"Beauty!",
"Beloved earth!"
Sometimes simply "Look, look here."

     Remember this as you turn to the rustle of branches
in the breeze. Perhaps the mudpeople have written a
message for you there? Are you listening? Do you want to
hear more?

     And names!
Names for each individual thing be it a snowflake,
    a grain of sand
or an entire lifetime.
For the mudpeople
names
are expressive of all the individual's past
and the future they have the potential to make.
They express one's purpose
or essence
as a name should.

The mudpeople can write your name with
      flowers and some stars,
on the backs of dolphins
or the wave cut by a hawk's wing.
They use
everything
to form the words
and so can call to us
each and all individually.
And though this says much of the new world
      I assumed upon waking,
much is still left to be discovered.

      My first days fill up with
      wonder and questions and learning.
Their talk is new to me,
but not foreign
and I pick up quickly
on their meanings,
their humor and guidance.
I struggle to pronounce their names as they say them.
But they are generous
about this
and allow me to fashion
some means of calling them
that comes more easily to my rough tongue.
My most constant companion at this time,
I call "Liet"
and it is quite some length of days

e
✳
•

before the laughter ceases
whenever I use this address.

     It is Liet who called me out on the first night,
stepping from under the play of shadow and light
to reveal to me the gig passing through my woods.
I learn later of the heavy bond
this places upon
a member of the genG,
as it is not a matter to be taken lightly.
To call out a crow
such as myself
entails responsibilities
and to do so
well past the equinox,
as Liet has done in my case,
is all the more demanding.

     For now
our path takes us to the west and south
to milder climes and easier trails.
Each day I grow stronger,
shed my old life, its ways and meanings,
and take on the way of the path before me,
eating new foods, learning new syllables and
     signs, filling my senses with new wonder.

     I travel with Liet
who walks among those who travel more
     widely and at times camp apart from the rest
     of the gig.
Such a group of companions

is called "the wag"
and each gig
is comprised,
like a ligature,
of the wag and the rillim.
These latter
are those who
are uninterested or unable to take to
the wandering paths
that parallel, intersect and dance
along the steadier line to the ancient places for
    camping, resting and story-telling.
The rillim may include
those undergoing some healing,
the young and elder-elders,
though one can spend days
with the wag running
beside genG of great age
with babes clinging to their backs.

    We run on ahead,
return to the rillim to camp
and set out again
in a rhythm
of curiosity,
happy surprise
and fulfillment.
We find stories and tell them
to ourselves and each other
by moonlight,
firelight
and with eyes wide

shut in sun
upon fields of snow.
I grow
to know
a handful of those who follow
Liet
and share with them the path and its seasons deep
with mystery.

Will the spring ever come?

There is Tibuktu
with the long memory
and stories
of many days' play
that sustain us
in the grey lands of bare deciduous
we travel through
to find the warmth along the equator.
It is Tibuktu who tells me
of the vast time
long before trees had come to be rooted into
    the earth in one place.
Of how then
Cedar and Willow, Oak and Elm
took to the path themselves
with the genG
and created with grand sweeping gestures
landscapes and hillside stands, glades and forests.

What a time of earth that must have been!
The mudpeople, the great acacia and giant sequoia
    walking the path side by side
in full stride
broadcasting tales and fables of great deeds and delights
into the wind
and back again
over the land.

And there is Shawadj.
An avid player
of *Ever-Not-Ever*,
Shawadj would eagerly reveal to me
those strategies
required
to glean the most from this inscrutable game.
Unfortunately, I am
a poor recipient of such wisdom
unable to grasp simultaneously
its variables
and its elegance.
In essence, *Ever-Not-Ever*
is a celebration
of the close bond between the mudpeople and
    lady bugs, *coleopterra: coccinellidae.*
Shawadj confides to me
how
the spots of lady bugs,
their very relation and configuration contain

messages passing from one genG to another.
It seems to me
a bit like the way
chess is played
through the mail.
The dots are encryption.
They communicate moves, the unfolding
    of cunning plans.
But unlike postal chess,
the genG don't address
the dots painted on the wings of the virgin's beetle
to some particular member
of some distant gig.
For the lady bugs, too,
are players in this game
and take these markings wherever they will.
It is up to
everyone involved
both lady bug and genG alike,
to grasp and utilize this spontaneity.
In this regard,
Ever-Not-Ever begins to resemble the improvisations
of jazz musicians
(though the genG do not make music
as it
is too close to number and mathematics.)
There is no real "winner"
or some one triumphant over all the others –
this would always come
down to some
lady bug
and they have no real regard for such trivial

things as winning and losing.
The best I can make out
is that everything means something
but what it means
is completely
mirrored
by our bewilderment
at any given moment.
Yet
throughout the game
there are
far
moments of great cleverness and surprise.
And so
whenever a lady bug appears
it is always a whisper
of magic,
bringing tidings from another world, something to
marvel and cherish.

Klee,
with wide eyes
and serene smile
like a contented child,
is also with us.
I walk beside Klee's
vast love of color,
among the light and the waves
of spectrums visible

and invisible
and feel pale.
But I must say
there was a day
I learned from this
how to be
the most tenuous translucency
of thick
rich
yellow-
green
and then heard Klee
say
"Color and I are one!"
I understood for that clean moment
the meaning of colors
and how shallow
my grasp of it will always be
held back
by biology
and symbolism and the eternal wheel.

Then laughing
and running on ahead
of even those who run on ahead
is Ril Walker, Liet's favorite.
Mercurial and exquisite
we most often see
only

the back of Ril Walker.
It is Ril Walker who shows us all the best places
and guides us to vistas
overflowing with breadth and beauty and potentiality.
Ril Walker holds the map
to the labyrinth,
looks daily into the eyes of the winged
    Nike of Samothrace
and sets out to teach me
the depths of all the earth's waters and
    their very buoyancy.

    We travel together,
form a close bond,
depend upon
one another,
share our gifts for the path.
It is a fluid arrangement
as are all relationships among the mudpeople.
Each individual
must chose for themselves the path they take
and all offer their help along this way.
One need not remain with the rillim or with the wag
or with the gig for that matter,
if time has come
for them to move on.
Indeed
most mudpeople spend
the entirety of their days within

the gig to which they are delivered,
walking the same paths through lands in their
    appointed season and rhythm.
But it is not required,
expected or even desired
of any member.
They must go where the story takes them
and if this be
to the Great Path itself,
the one that goes round this world entire,
all of the gig
and all of the gigs upon the earth
are respectful.

    Liet, a bright light of the people,
walks as one called to the Great Path
and I am keenly aware of this mark upon
    my companion.
Our gig,
especially those among the wag,
devote much to the preparations this requires.
The elders call forth from all the gig the stories
    of their being.
These are given
to walk with Liet in the lone way of the Great Path.
And so advice on the best means
to read
the signs along the path
is exchanged and discussed.
Tales that describe how to find food,
    clean water and healing mudbaths are offered.
Continuous debates on

the pros and cons
of lignum vitae,
dream interpretation,
nature vs. nurture,
rhyming schemes,
the suspected triviality of true propositions,
the DH rule,
and more,
much, much more
are to be heard
as we travel,
camp,
sleep,
and wake to travel again south and west.
Others share the lessons
written under stones,
scribbled through tunnels
and marked on
the rippling lakeshores
that tell of weather to come
and the lay of the land ahead.
In quiet whispers
I hear talk
far off
of Meme and Shtsch-Ha.

Though Liet may join the Fey-fi
and walk the Feya-fi,
this is not considered to be
some right of birth or mark of privilege.
The Fey-fi are honored and esteemed
Imagine the stories they must tell!

but not envied.
One does not owe them allegiance
or obedience
like the royalty
or elected officials of our history.
Such deference is held
only for the path itself
and the stories of its unfolding.
One is meant to follow the path, Fey-fi or no,
and for the genG,
all is ordered by this happy dictum of life.
As the Fey-fi have their path,
so, too, the gig walks the one they have been given.
It takes both
and all their stories
to bring this world
each day around again
into the sun.
By this
all are made equal in their going.

    It will take all these stories
and the many yet to be told
to sustain Liet in the life on the Feya-fi.
I feel a deep sense of awe
to be the small
witness I am to it.

Though the company of
Liet and these companions is a
deep joy to me,
among all that walk beside Liet I am drawn
most to Scout.
Dark and unusually silent for genG,
Scout is believed
to have once been Fey-fi
and often is the lead for the wag.
Perhaps too old to walk the Great Path any longer
(though age among mudpeople cannot be determined),
I sense some
something
heavy with weight and reckoning
in this one
when on rare nights
stories from dreams spill out of Scout
as unstructured and unstoppable as idioms.
I am drawn to this darkness and wait with it,
listen for the answers to questions of the future
yet to come.
It is Scout
who tells me of my name. It is Scout
who is the first at my mudding.

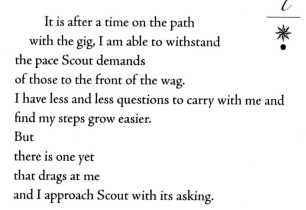

It is after a time on the path
   with the gig, I am able to withstand
the pace Scout demands
of those to the front of the wag.
I have less and less questions to carry with me and
find my steps grow easier.
But
there is one yet
that drags at me
and I approach Scout with its asking.

   "What is my name?"
"You are known as 'Crow.'"
"But many of these here are called 'Crow.'
With all the alphabet and alphabets
open to you,
to the genG,
creators of all alphabets,
why does this one word do so much?"

   Scout looks out
to some distant horizon
and draws back from it an answer.

   "Long ago,
in the beginning,
when the genG first walked the earth,
it is true
they created the alphabet

and named all things
and set them down.
With this first taste
and this first breath
of this power of logos,
they also fell into the making of number.
For a time all was well.
Stories were told far and wider;
many profound and timeless themes and styles
    developed.
But then came a time when strife broke out
and many fought among themselves,
each claiming ownership for the multiplicity of things,
like cups,
walking staffs,
even stories.
And some among the genG began
to set themselves up as better than
others.

        The great wise ones among the mudpeople
saw this happening
and determined that the cause of all this evil
and ill will
was the presence
and use
of number
in our culture.
So, to return to the old ways
and to the happinesses they had loved and known,
the mudpeople rid themselves of number,
cast it aside by the riverside
and walked on.

Along came Crow.
And you know
how dearly crows
love bright and shiny objects.
And there is nothing brighter or shinier than number.
Seeing such sparkle down by the riverside,
washing and twinkling in the clear riverbed,
Crow could not resist
and rushed down to take what was thought to be
    a bright prize.
It was not long before Crow realized
the deceit and evil caused by number
and wanted to give it back.
But the mudpeople would not take number back
and to this day,
crows follow in the wake of gigs,
searching for mudpeople
to give back to them the numbers they invented.
And that is why crows always are crying,
complaining
that they have been so cursed
to be weighed down by the bright and shiny
    evil of numbers.

It is from this ancient myth of my people
that you,
and those like you,
are named 'Crow'
for you follow us like crows do
and come from a world that is still filled
by number and its evil.
But in calling you 'Crow',

we remind ourselves also
that we have made you
and some of the troubles that lay in your path.
Someday,
as all the genG know,
we must return to that riverside
and destroy once and for all the evil we have created
    and set loose in this world,
or continue to be cursed
and denied
forever
the full presence
of Meme, our soul and god."

            The weight of this story is
            with me for many days
and I fall back
to take up with the rillim.
Days are warmer there somehow
and nights are sweet smelling.
Soon I am lightened.
But before I can return
to take up the path with the wag among Liet,
    Scout and the others,
there is one more step to be taken.

        I know my name
and how that lays with the genG.

I know that my place is among them.
But the last line back to my old life unravels
    only with my mudding.
It is there and then
that I begin
to be forever
a foreigner to my old life and yet a supplicant
    to my present.
It is there and then
that I begin to be at one
with the mudpeople and their way in the world.
This dizzying baptism
of mud and frenzied Tingeltangel Yab-Yum
cuts me loose
and propels me like a newborn into a world
brave
and new
and achingly elusive
like water through my fingers.
I can keep none of it and will not give any of it back.

How to
hold on to
delight
and insight
and aufgehoben?

It is like this at my mudding:

The fires of our camping are bright and warm.
They make me sleepy in their glowing.
I close

my eyes
and hear stories all about me as the gig settles in
to the night.
There is laughter
and hushed greeting,
secretive and scheming.
I hear many of the wag with us, among them
    Liet and our companions.
And though I feel
content to lean
against a juniper at some remove from the
    center of activities and traffic,
I am filled
with a building indeterminate itch
that must be scratched
but defies
satisfaction.
It is exquisite to me,
like the very talisman of changes I have undergone,
and its pleasure grows
more so
the longer I withhold from the relief of it.

    I press into the rough
of the tree's trunk
and consider my clothes against my skin.
The days have worn them and torn them.
I do not know where or when
I lost my shoes.
I suppose
these clothes
are the source of my crawling discomfort

and I scrape my back against the juniper again.
Still there is no relief.

The fires' scent comes to me,
bringing its embrace and confidence.
I smile.

Then somewhere
there
is a shriek of delight off in the woods.
My eyes
snap open to search for the mischief
only to find
Scout's firm warm hands wrapped around my ankles.
We smile,
laugh loud.
There is a rough tug
and I am dragged from the juniper's roots
delighted and leering,
kicking and screaming.
The entire gig is in on it.
Soon
we are all
tumbling down the hillside
in the moonlight
pushing and pulling each other to the river's edge
into the mud that waits for us all there.

The viscous goo
sucks us in
to Itself.
I am up to my neck in it giggling and weeping

like a child in a pillow fight.
It is manic
with innocence
and pleasure
and sweet surprises.
My tattered rags are a problem no more.
They are gone and I,
like the rest of the gig,
am stitchless,
naked,
nude.

When this frenzied night is complete
I will be shown
how to mix and apply
the requisite recipes
of loam
and liquid
to protect my skin
from the whimsy of the path
and maintain my body temperature whatever
    the season.
To be free
of zipper and buttons,
sleeves
and waistbands
is heaven
and I am
wild to be without them.

Imagine voices low and high,
screeching and roaring like a stampede

in a roiling mass of muddied glistening
flesh of every sex.
The moonlight is filled with us.
There is no holding back,
no separation of oneself from the other,
no unhappiness
whatsoever.
We are all throbbing
with desire
and the fulfillment of desire.

Imagine.

Everything
slips and slides easily out and in.
The whole world seems to be nothing
but tongues and tangle.
There is no coming
up for air;
there is no breathing.
It is
as if
we have all been turned into liquid or light and
only Heraclitus presides.

Imagine how it is to be the center of all things. Wisha!

This should sound familiar
even to you.
You may have heard tell of housewives and maidens
screaming from the forests,

running, tripping over their raked garments.
Found half-mad with tales of kidnappings in the woods.
Many crows flee
from their mudding
and stumble back to their settlements in such a state.
By the time the authorities can collect an understanding,
the gig is long gone and never to be found.
Many a priest and dowager
have quit their brief sojourn with the
    mudpeople on the night of their mudding,
unable to discard their wits
with their garments
and step into the rushing waters
of this consuming frenzy
even once.

    Scout finds me among the coil
of sighing limbs
and wild eyes
and leads me aside
and away.
I follow, sliding
weak-kneed
and as open as a freshly bloomed flower.
Mud is everywhere
into all my pores and crevices.
As it dries,
it pulls at me even while
my renewed aroused desire

pushes at my expanding flesh.
This is maddening and delightful
and beyond
denial.
I
am a crawling mad appetite.

We stumble into a nearby stand of pines
and lay down in the soft fresh needles among
      bright winking stars.
Scout's hands begin
their searching and slow persuasion,
painting finely etched symbols into the mud canvas
      that is my eager body.
I flex my arched back,
ask
into the meaning
of each rune
scrawled across my torso,
limbs
and throbbing skin.
Every reply a perfect question.

      Boom,
Boom,
Boom,
Boom;
How-How-How-How.

      My fingers blaze,
trace limbs
and curves curious to discover what my partner

is made of.
Though the genG travel "clothed" in
only their mud-streaked skin,
there is no easy way to read an individual's sex.
This may seem suspect,
naive,
but it would require that one stare
and this would make me
far more uneasy than any
focus of my attention.
But now
in this whirl and dance of coition,
I am initiate to even
this mystery
and share with Scout
full knowledge.

    Eagerness
and rapt attention to our present endeavor together
is more alluring to me
than the considerable skill and originality
of cat and mouse we manage to display for each other.
I drive on,
pounding,
crashing
and squirming
to hold
and mold
myself
into that single
quizzical
shape

of writhing flesh
that asks for only "More?"

    Scout makes a flower box of every
   intersection of my flesh
and soon
even the sky
is written with the word "Yes!"
And I am falling happily
into every exhausted spent
consonant
and vowel available.

    We lay together
and watch as Time itself dances
with the most exquisite angel
on the head of a pin.
There is no beginning, no middle or end.
And then
I leave the pool of my mudding
and begin a Damascus way of being.
So many things possible,
so many things in their place,
unburdened
and unknown to the world.
I feel free
to create myself anew every
minute.

    This is
what power is.

In the morning,
as the wag gathers to take to the path,
I seek Liet to share the change in me.
From a tense fist of elder-elders,
the familiar voice like the song of sunrise,
confident and strong, replies
"We will address this later.
Crow's mudding still vibrates among us. Let's celebrate
it."

Then
a darkening cloud in somber timbre
cuts through like suspicion,
"Your time is soon. The Great Path calls and
    you must be ready."
"The Feya-fi calls but I choose it. It is my path
    and no other determines the shape of its going."
"We have not met here to be taught the ways
    of our own people.
The path for elder-elders is just as clear. This Crow is
    of concern. You jeopardize much, too much.
    Not just for yourself but for the gig as well.
Will you choose another from among us to guide
    this one so that you may be free?
I must tell you we are not eager for this responsibility.
This Crow spends too much time with you among the
    wag and looks to burn out."
"Then I will not accept another guide. It sounds as if
you have already marked Crow for abandonment."

"Well, tell us, how much *kimiya* have you had to use?
    Are you still using it?"
"Only on that first night. Doesn't that tell you
    something of the spirit here?
Abandonment would be wrong.
I sense a great story in this one.
Let us speak no more of this. I choose; this is the path."

    Liet leaves their company
unaware
that I am witness to their talk.
But the eyes of elder-elders fall upon me
and the magic of my mudding
is gone under their stare.
I feel chilled and naked.

    Among the wag this day I am heavy and avoid
Liet.

    We are set to camp apart
    from the rillim.
This lightens my feeling
as I am not keen
to share fires in the company of the elders.
Liet seeks me out and takes me aside.
Scout joins us with a bright step and scheming eye.
"It is time for you to play some mischief with us.
Keep your eyes open.

Be as silent as you can.
And stay close by."

"Where are we going? I don't understand.
Am I to be abandoned?"

Liet startled, turns,
"What have you heard?
Never mind; that is not for you to consider.
Dismiss it.
It is a path we will not be traveling.
Come.
Enjoy this night. Now.
How
can you ignore the poetry that fills this very moment?
Feel it pulse? Feel it beating?
Feel the trees and the rustling between them?
The earth turning to the sun again?
We ride towards the solstice tonight and take
    word of this into the world.
Breathe it in with us
and let's make mischief.
Yes?
Then we go. So, follow!"

Liet's speech pulls me
forward into the conspiracy.
We are met by a small band from the wag
and silently all
run through tall grasses
and reeds of the marshland surrounding the bayou.

Our feet race and clamor,
splashing and crashing,
into the shallow water's edge.
This sounds to some
like a running
school of fish or
an alligator
hunting.
But we easily
pass over their sentry
and soon
come out onto
short neat rows of homes
sleepy and secure.
These will be
our booty.

    The group divides.
Liet, Scout and I
head for a modest home steeped in the dead of night
locked up tight
against the dark
and the fear of the dark.
We easily enter in.
It does not take
any breaking
or forcing.
There is an incantation —
you know the one
from childhood —
that at least one lock on every dwelling is partial to.
It quickly gives up its grip

and admits us
blushing.

     Inside
is orderly and well-kept.
You can sense
some measure of the inhabitants' pride
from its cozy happiness.
It feels peaceful though stiff,
as if lacking an essential wildness,
that cries out for the gift of our visit.

     I am awed by our audacity.
We roam through their home
undefended,
undetected,
free and easy,
curious about their small precious treasures,
reading their mail,
petting their pets —
among them a yellow dog,
tail
wagging and anxious to please.
Oh, I forget
how much I miss such company
and stoop to nuzzle his neck so sweet and domestic.

     Soon
we are into
the drawers and the closets.
Liet and Scout stop to run
their palms over the cotton,

the silk,
300 count, 600 count percale,
flannel and flowered.
All are devoured
in their rapt caress.
Bed linens are a weakness with mudpeople.
I have seen them stilled for what seems hours
    among freshly cleaned sheets;
content and motionless,
hypnotized
by their wonder of a culture that could be so wise
as to devise
bed clothes.

Now
when you lay down
of a hot summer's night,
tucked in tight,
your toes wriggling in
to every hospital corner,
there,
that pool of coolness
there in the deep recess,
that is their legacy
left for you,
a chilling reminder,
yes?
of the mudpeople's shrouded presence.

Scout wanders about the house
searching
and passes into the child's room,

hovers over the kindred innocence there
and settles into
whispering
low
gentle
dreamy
stories.
These sound like branches scratching the window.
These sound like frogs and bugs working in the night.
These sound like the filling for plush toys.
When junior wakes
and takes
these tales to school,
the words will tumble,
tongue-tied
and incoherent like babble.
Poor, dear, misunderstood child.

    It is like this when you can't remember clearly
      your dreams.
In your head,
they feel vivid.
But your tongue cannot paint
the shapes
the mudpeople have left for you in there.

Liet and I are in the master
bedroom suite.
bedroom suite.
Mr. and Mrs.
deep in sleep
do not dream.
Filled with bills,
the banking, the shopping, the heat and the washing,
drilled by a constant stream
of headlines
and deadlines
and expert advice
on how to fix
the leak in the basement,
what to mix
into the meatloaf,
stock picks
and speeding tickets,
there is no room in this room
for dreams or intimacies,
for confidences or privacy.

Immediately
Liet calls a sweet breeze
in through
the window
and we are all stirred by it.
Mr. and Mrs. shift in their sheets,
sigh,
settle back in again.
All the while

my companion
to the singsong rhythm
of a naughty incantation
performs the antidote for all this poison.

      The remote is removed beyond reach.
It will be found one day
many months away
among the laundry.
Tubes are taken from the bath cabinet.
Vanishing cream vanishes.
44 Greeks form a chorus line
and serpentine
down the drain.
Brushes, combs, and razor blades
parade
across the ceiling
and disappear
into thin air
in the far corner.
Circuits are rewired in the clocks and the radios.
Alarms will not be
summoning
any
one
tomorrow morning.

      I dance to these pranks and pleasures.
Filled with their spirit
I hit
the closet.
I find

all his ties
and all her pantyhose
and arrest them for crimes
against nature.
They are sent to Liet for sentencing.
The ties are hung by the neck 'til dead;
the pantyhose are drawn and quartered.
Our justice is wit
and the case is soon dismissed
with this final judgment:
DON'T GO
INTO WORK TOMORROW
OR ALL THIS WEEK.
TELL THEM YOU ARE SICK.
TELL THEM YOU HAVE AN APPOINTMENT.
TELL THEM YOU HAVE NOTHING
    TO WEAR;
CAN'T DO A THING WITH YOUR HAIR.
TELL THEM YOU HAVE MYSTERIOUSLY
    MISPLACED ALL YOUR UNDERWEAR.

    Now it is time to go.
Liet fluffs the pillows,
kisses each on the cheek,
pinches their soft hips,
and sets one last charm loose
in the air above their bed
to hover over their heads
from the ceiling.
The words trickle down,
all smiles,
entwining Mr. and Mrs.

in groggy giggles and kisses.
When we set out from this house,
love is in the air.

    Our raiding band gathers.
We come together to huddle around a small dirt hole
and each donates some piece
of stolen domesticity;
a single sock,
a watch,
this month's phone bill;
a set of keys,
an abused Barbie,
some little black book;
phone messages,
homework pages,
cigarettes and matches.
All find their place,
slide in with each other
and fill up the space.
We'll hide these.
Maybe some bulldozer
will pull them up
in an effort to expand the neighborhood.
Or, a future archeologist discovers these
and weaves
a story of his own.
Maybe we'll return someday
and bring them back to their owners,
then gather up others,
new and improved.
Though their absence

be a nuisance
and a bit frustrating,
maybe some lives need changing.
And so some gift of Spontaneity
is given by taking.

    As we walk back into the night
away
from the cluster of homes we've raided,
I ask into all
the causes —
final,
material,
efficient,
and formal,
of our play and mischief.
"Can I do that?
Mix and match
charms and chants,
and make any inanimate object dance?
Can I
visit them
and those like them
in the night?
Even in bright daylight?
Can I
give and take
from those asleep or awake
dreams

and wonders
and pieces of small plunder?
Can I learn these things,
to look into the soul of every being,
see
the meaning
deep within
and charm
and chant
and laugh again
and again?"
"Yes, some.
Some of it you may know.
It is for you to know and I will show you.
But understand, these
are not powers conferred on you by me;
these are necessities of initiation
into the mysteries
of Story.
For when you
learn to
look into
the eye of all creation
and withdraw from there
the words
of power,
then you will be the creator
of your own story.
Then you will see how the path is littered
with nouns
and pronouns,
modifiers and verbs,

articles,
conjunctions,
karawane,
and slang.
They stretch out from this place and every other
like a crossword puzzle
unending,
unfinished,
ever-changing and filled with promise.
When you know this
you will find where your story lies,
you will know why there is no answer,
you will hear the history of all time
on the horizon
coming for you,
and you will overhear
your story whisper
to itself
deep wisdom.
There is this great story in you, Crow.
Let us go
find it."

And so
I am brought into
the circle around the fires of our camping.
The gig gathers there
to tell tales of their going
and each evening
begins:

"To stand
under a yellow tree,
imagining."
The telling of this beloved story,
the most beloved and the most honored
of all the stories of the mudpeople,
is a celebration
shared among all those at the fire.
Its telling is passed from one to another,
to my left,
to my right,
night after night.
Its sweetness expressed in the sweet voice of this one;
its suspense and grace
exposed by that.
Each time it is new
and its meaning developed
as the days unfold and envelop us
"...under a yellow tree,
imagining."

Following this call like a call to prayer,
we encircle the fire
to share
its warmth
and offer our stories.
Some are standards,
told many times.
Some are new,
those whose origin
is right there and then.
Stories are told one after the other

and so on
as the stars progress across the sky.
This string of stories
(*Beautiful! Beautiful words!*)
is called "novel" and
as you can
imagine
some nights are filled with astounding sequences.
This is part
of the "game" or "art"
of novel —
to wait for just the right moment
to call out your story,
to try to predict who will follow yours,
and so on
into the night.
Some may claim
that this form takes its name
from French,
from the 15th century.
But the French word is from another word
and all the words are given from the genG.
Many of the great works of that other world in
    this form
are taken directly or in part from
such nights as these,
for many great Crow authors have walked
    among the genG,
received training from them
and taken stories from them.
I shall not name them here.
It is cruel.

And besides the mudpeople
do not consider novels theirs or some individual's.
They are all a gift from Meme.
Let them be told.

      Oh, how I wish you
could stare into
the fire in the clearing,
smell the pines by the pond,
hear their voices gathering and
ascending and
witness when they light upon
legends
and themes,
mysteries
and mythologies
and from all these
weave
a song of long going!

      To stand
under a yellow tree,
imagining.
(*Now it's your turn.*

_____

_____

_____ *fill in your story here.*
Or anywhere.
Or choose from

some
I remember by heart:)

Into the clearing, light spilled
and painted a shadow there for night to fill.

They came up the hill slowly, carrying.

Neither rain nor sleet nor threat of snow
can keep me from my appointed rounds.

Someone. We

Her knees winked at me.

If you come to a fork in the road, take it.

And I said
Yes I will Yes.

I love you.

The mason's finger
bleeds
near azaleas.

My little fingers and small hands
could not hold on to
the faith that was my mother.

And I could not see for seeing.

Amen.

Have you heard them before?
Do these sound familiar?
Do you remember?
Do you?

These are just a few and
   there are many more
to pass between us in the blaze of the fire.
I grow accustomed
to some
of the rhythm,
word configuration,
and grammatical manipulation.
It is dizzying.
Over time
whole days are spent
in service to a single story.
And such a story!
The only requirement — that it not be
too heavy to carry.
Now every curve line of the path
opens to reveal to me
words,
phrases,
happy endings.
I collect them all,
bring them to Liet
and we cull through them for delights.
We are often together,

inseparable,
constructing,
deconstructing,
arguing,
brow to brow.
We try on words,
look for them
like entries in a thesaurus
across vast stretches,
unpack their meanings,
their voices,
their poetry.
It is a time of enchantment.
I am at one with myself,
with the dear earth,
with the path that lies before me.
I feel as if I know everything I need to know.
But even knowing is known
for the shallow thing it is.

    Liet turns to me,
"Wait 'til you see High Solstice.
How do I describe it?
It is
extravagance.
It is
abundance.
It is the whole world at our finger tips.
What grand days of bright, continuous
story-making-story-telling.
We are set for that site
and will reach there soon.

Soon
the genG in all their most glory
will gather and become one
each giving their appointed portion
that drives this world from its beginnings.
The great festival
is greater than the soul of any novel.
It is genius.
It is spontaneous.
It is the ecstasy of the saints.
And we are then genuine-true-to-life!
You must see this.
More, you must be part of it.
Prepare your story
and we will introduce it."

      With all the world before me a *tabula rasa,* I set
out to find
any sign or semiotic,
any word,
phrase
or bit of punctuation
that may produce for me
an introduction
at High Festival.
I scour the countryside, watch
patiently for days
the blades of grass,
the play of sun and rain
on pasture,
hill,
road

and valley.
Rocks are arranged
and rearranged;
boxes are drawn in the sand on the shore.
These will not do.
I leave them all just as they are
and search wider still.
When I am done
with these alphabets
and phonetics,
I am still empty.
Ex nihilo, nihil fit.

      I turn for consolation
to endless fits
of nightly mischief.
Long since that first
I have developed my skills
to come and go
through houses and homes
at my leisure.
It is there among that sleepy predictable domesticity
I find companions
who ask nothing of me.
No rhyme,
no reason,
and definitely,
no story,
but receive me with such unfathomable brotherhood.
I am always welcome
and refreshed by their rapt devotion.
I have gone to the dogs literally in my frustration.

From these there is one,
one special one,
I call "Sudden."
She is the color of peanut butter
and of questionable origin but true
and I am unable to
deny myself her fidelity.
The path seems to loosen its demands on me
when I am with Sudden.

And in time
we together, this one and I,
in the darkest hours before the light,
hunt down and tree
my story.
It comes down around me
full force
fully formed,
inspired and happy.
We
work on it,
get it right,
get it just right,
and head out at breaking daylight
with it tucked tight in my soul.
Sudden follows.

You may have your talents and skills.
You may have the approval
of your teachers and the authorities.
But I have an original
idea.

On the way back to the
camp and to the gig,
Sudden and I are followed by
shadows
darker than dark.
They nag at me.
Are they doubts?
Are they fears?
Are they the punctured exaltations
that stalk every act of creation?
I turn to face them,
to stare them down
and am startled to look into eyes
warm, filled with surprise
and generous wisdom.
"Who are you?"
I want to know.
"Well, Crow, never mind that but let us go
back to your camp together.
You have been gone too long
this night."
I no longer feel alarm
and am at ease in their presence.
Somehow it is magnificence
to return with both my story
and such creatures as these.

"Crow, where have you been?"
Liet steps out from the crowd.
"And who is that with you? Such a pretty

thing...and friendly, too."
Sudden's cold nose seeks Liet's sensitive places.
"Who more?
Some brethren of the Great Path? You bring us Fey-fi?
How clever!"
"We were on our way to High Festival,
as you are as well,
and were following a Muse.
She lead us to this one
and then departed.
Our path apparently goes in this direction."
"A Muse?
That's what's different about you, Crow.
Yes, I see now. Look, look at the eyes
and all through the hair.
There is something of the glow of Inspiration there.
How are you feeling?"
"Hungry, but unable to eat.
Dizzy
and sleepy
and full of energy,
like I'm buzzing.
Confused mostly, I think."
"Yes, that is to be expected.
You must go lie down and sleep.
We will call you when it is time."
"But..."
"Don't resist. Go. When you wake, we will say more of
this. Go."

These Fey-fi remain with us
through the days leading to High Solstice.

Their strangeness is
impenetrable to me;
their way of speech, their tongue and rhythm,
too abstract and foreign.
One night around the fire,
one of them
calls us all to gather in
and I swear
the Yellow Tree Itself appears
without a sound.
They are dark and animal-like,
though not like any animals I have known,
domestic or feral,
but like mythical animals,
unpredictable and powerful with an instinctual
intelligence, visionary.
But, in spite of this,
it is their gracefulness and their deep happiness
that draws me to them and their company.
They are welcoming.
I sit
to watch and to listen
and can
only take in
small ephemeral portions.
Their stories they seem to speak to themselves
    or to the earth itself.
They are always of *terra alma.*

How to grasp the mystic's vision?
Words?
These words?

A miracle, Yes!
Yet nevertheless
a prison.

    The Fey-fi walk the Feya-fi,
the great path that goes round this blue globe.
They carry with them
the vision of the world entire.
It is a vision given them
by Shtsch-ha, the mother of all.
It is she who was the first to follow the path.
It is Shtsch-ha who drew the streams
down the hillside and out to the seas.
It is she who thought up dreams.
Shtsch-ha is the mother of all,
honored and loved,
and in some places she is called
"the blue lady."
It is Shtsch-ha who gives stories their poetry.

    And the Great Path,
the Great Path goes round the earth
in many different directions.
Generally these run
parallel to the equator
or take a more perpendicular course
North and South.
Each has its treacheries, its perils and wonders.
Those routes walked by this or that Fey-fi
are read easily
from the strings of beads displayed around the ankle.
Green beads mean they go East and West;

with blue, they move
North to South / South to North.
Of the Fey-fi who walk to High Solstice with us
there is one who stands apart,
the one who is the darkest,
called "Ha-ah."
The beads on this one fascinate me.
Each one is unique.
Some sparkle,
some are etched with minuscule runes,
some filled with roots and precious liquids.
Such ornaments are maps and charts of the
    course taken.
To read their meanings is a story long and heavy.
It tells of WAR,
FAMINE,
the wealth of UNHAPPINESS and SORROW
of the world.
It promises peace
and sanctuary, an ending in light and love.
It feels a bit like madness
better glimpsed in the distance from above.
And I have too little skill to withstand an
    understanding of it.

    Instead I am lost to practicalities.
I want to know how it is possible to go round the earth
walking.
Surely it must be
mixed with sailing
or flying —
all that water, how to get over the water?

But they insist:
there is only one mode of travel for the genG —
walking,
one foot in front of the other
upon the earth.
Bicycles,
boats,
trains,
cars —
these are deemed absurdities
for the point is not to get there faster or on time.
As for flying —
absolutely
out of the question.
While cars and trains may be absurd, amusing even,
flying is worse than dying.
It can scarcely be comprehended.
It is Meaninglessness Itself.
To be so separated from all that is good in this life,
to be removed from the earth,
all that gives their lives value and meaning,
is a soul-destroying horror
not to be considered.

      Besides there is no need to be flying.
The Feya-fi stretches out over vast oceans
and any body of water.
You may have glimpsed it
in the line of moonlight or sunrise from
your point on the shore out to the horizon.
It goes beyond,
round the world entire

and the genG walk it,
walk on the waters,
following,
trailing their footprints behind
among the ripples of the tide.

    Are you not familiar with stories of those
      who part the waters to cross to the other side?
Or those who walk upon the water itself?
Why should there not be other stories of a people
    who, too, can do that?
Who possess that magic and that faithfulness?
And though it be magic to them,
all the mudpeople possess it
and can wield it.
It is as familiar and as easy to them as imagination.
Yet it, too, is an art, a thing of much beauty and awe.

    The Fey-fi walk the Feya-fi, the great path
      that goes round this blue globe,
entire.

    The site for High Solstice
is yet a few days' distance
from our camp.
I scramble frantically,
prepare myself, rehearse the story,
gather my resources.

"But how will I know when it is my turn to go?"
"The story will tell itself, you'll see.
Don't worry."
But I do worry
and wonder
and become
a jumble
of giddy energy.
I am filling with the spirits of the gods,
enthused.
All my senses humming,
awake
and running into every crevice of the present.
All the gig feels this, too.
Our path is psychedelic, electrified.
You cannot miss it.
The excitement smells like lemons.
Our dreams at night are contagious
and as bright as daylight.
Colors are everywhere smiling back at us.
My mind,
my soul
and will are one.
The gig is my body.

Bring it on!

Liet turns to me,
"You are ready. You are.
This will be such a High Solstice
as we have not seen in many years, I'm sure.
Your first!

Oh, I envy you.
I remember my first for story-making-story-telling.
So long ago, so full and overflowing,
and blessed surely in the presence of Meme.
Such magic, I can't tell you.
A time of clarity and mystery.
And then to be under the yellow tree,
to witness the Fey-fi weave, unravel and weave
the power of the lily soliloquy...!"

    The entire world seems to sigh with the
    mention of this.
The Fey-fi among us draw up to their full height,
throw their heads back slowly, gracefully
unfolding
smiles into closed eyes.
Somewhere there is a crow call against the rock
    face of a mountain wall.
I feel my heart
stop.

    Liet exhales
and again
exhales,
arms stretched out, palms down,
begins
to give a halting description
of the beauty called "the lily soliloquy."
"The Fey-fi gather in,
there may be many or some,
odd or even,
sometimes one.

I like it best when they are even.
They weave through a dance in unison,
each in a unique distinct direction,
each move a complete compliment of the moves
    of the others;
like continents whirling through space
in orbit around a sun
in orbit around a fixed point of pure imagination.
Such rhythm.
But more than rhythm and more than the words —
though the words are in
the essential language;
they are the soul's interpretation
of its soul;
they are the face of happiness.
When all the Fey-fi gathered in
extend their arms towards the horizon,
it is as if whole worlds unfold from their brows
to pool around
their long feet. It is like being present at the creation.
I like it best when they are even.
Then the Fey-fi tell a story of walking
since before the time of Shtsch-ha."

This image hangs with us
all the way to High Solstice
and to the very roots of the yellow tree.
We have arrived at High Festival.
The shear force of so many mudpeople

transform most of my beliefs about the way of
    this world, its shape and size.
How could all these genG be among us
and yet go unnoticed?
They walk the path less traveled.
They must.
They guide camels through the eye of the needle.
They must.
They must vacation frequently
in the land of dreamy dreams.
But even this does not explain the crush of gigs
    gathered here
and all those assembled this very day everywhere
across the hemisphere.

        It is a small city.
People, and banners opening to the sky,
colors,
curves and angles,
surfaces of every kind,
languages, information,
gifts for the senses and delicacies from unknown places
as far as I can see.
These radiate from the roots of the yellow tree
whose massive broad shape rises
above the wide field of tall golden golden grasses.
Greetings and laughter,
shrill and deep,
lead us into the mass.
Everyone knows everyone
and everyone knows me.
I have never felt so warmly
welcomed.

Our band disbands.
Ril Walker takes off for the booth
displaying the favorite rain game "quq."
Already Shawadj is among the convention
of *Ever-not-Ever* players
easily spotted by the halo of lady bugs
that follow them wherever they go.
We soon leave Klee behind,
motionless and rapt
and head-over-heels immersed in
the vibration
of the yellow
of the yellow tree and its limbs.
Tibuktu is gone to check the enrollments
and to add our names to those who have arrived.
Ha-ah, Liet, Scout
and I with Sudden by my side,
head towards the center of this hive.

To take in all this is overwhelming.
I am helpless in its tidal energy.
I lack the filter familiarity with such a scene provides.
It is all
activity everywhere
all around me,
purposeful, directed, focused.
I am struggling
to find Scout's hand,
to hold on
to keep from sliding aside.
I am told to "Breathe. Breathe."
then the panic begins to fall from me.

We proceed and finally reach the base of the great tree.

All ye! All ye! Outs in free!

We are met here by those Fey-fi present this day
gathered in
and making ready for the novel to begin.
They are even
including Ha-ah and the others who have
    arrived with our gig.
I smile to think of Liet's happiness with this.
Liet who likes it best when
the Fey-fi are even.

I find a place among them
and slide in.
When I turn to my left,
a gasp is heard,
and I am looking into
the most beautiful blue face imaginable.
Blue,
all blue,
every hue of blue.
Is it she?
A name almost escapes my lips.
But no name,
no word
is heard.
Only fragments are available.
And before the language of thought itself is lost
I have the thought:

It is as fine a day as I have ever lived.

It is all confusion from here on in.

It is as if I am on my back in the sun,
looking directly up into blue sky.
Such full blue,
maybe all blue
and no clouds.
Maybe my thoughts are disguised as cumulus.
They float by and every drop of sun
that falls upon them
and the land below
leaves bright cells of perfect joy.
We are all gathered there,
you and I
and everyone ever,
pure
and complete.

Someone somewhere is about to speak.
It is the call.
It is the prayer.

"To stand under a yellow tree, imagining."

It is begun.

Immediately
there is hush.
First an elder-elder imagines
the arbitrary play of definitions;
next this humor
is raised to axioms
by another;
then some fairer of the Fey-fi
make a mirror of the Rosetta stone.
High Festival is opened.
The spell is cast.
The spell is broken.
The genG are masked and unmasked.
So the story goes
on.

The crowd presses at me;
Come!
Leave behind the need for plot,
for character development.
Put your finger in the middle of the middle
and follow it all the way to the vortex.
Open,
open,
open
the mouth of every word
in every language
and speak into it.
Call for Being,
the presence of the present tense

and then exist
more marvelous than any Cartesian Meditation.
Narro, sum.
Sum!
Sum!
Sum!

All day. (But what is day?)
All night. (Without knowing it is night.)
Hold on,
hold
a little longer,
until
the story comes
round
to
you!

And then
there I am
in the middle of the middle,
speaking in the tongue
that comes from
Sudden's muzzle,
reaching out with all that holds out
for her tail,
chasing it,
round and round,
exhausting exhaustion
to collapse
and spiral down,
down,

down,
as the next takes up my story,
casts it into the heavens,
to the south and west.
Sirius invisible howls
and descends
beneath the horizon
soon to be followed by the setting sun.
Still the tale wags on
in seemingly perpetual motion.

       At one point we are all playing peek-a-boo
with the moon;
your hands over my eyes,
my hands over yours,
and those to either side.
Liet appears
out of nowhere
with footnotes to light our way home.
We all follow them
to the place where Scout will tell of the creation
of a moment of silence,
perhaps even of remembrance itself.

       We are silent.

       There are so many stories this day (or is it days?)
They come from everyone everywhere.
Even Walt Whitman is here.
I don't remember them all;
I do not have the power to contain them all
though I contain multitudes

and am blessed with multitudes.
Of this there is no doubt.

   And before we are done
all the Fey-fi rise
and offer the lily soliloquy
and beauty has never been so beautiful.
The blue one,
the one whose name
I want to say
but do not say,
extends both hands
and these become
the blue hands of Meme.
And then the sky is holding us inside its palm
and all is brilliance forever.

   But the festival ends
as it must end,
as it is meant to end,
with the final story
when the one chosen
lights fire.
There may be fireworks
and conical hats,
Pentecostal apostles with burning hair.
Once an entire metropolis
was plunged into darkness
to reveal the single spark
we all breathed flame into.
Fire.
Flame.

Light.
Celebration.
All is more fabulous than my mudding,
more delicious than night mischief,
more exuberant than my first hours with the mudpeople.
I am a story-maker
and celebrated as one.
"Dog chasing tail" is now among the beloved.
I am told it will be told and re-told
at many festivals in the time to come.
I have given more than I have taken.
Congratulations!

But there are some places that are
not so yellow.

"Where
will you go now,
Crow?"
Suddenly I have stepped into deep shadow,
lost my bearings, wandered too far from the yellow tree.
I should know this voice but I do not know
    who is speaking or where it is coming from.
"What?," I ask.
"Liet leaves tomorrow
on the Great Path.
Where do you go?"
The shadow grows
thicker, crawls into my head,

takes up residence there
and hides happiness from me.

    It is like this when
Doubt begins
its whisper
and finds all manner of Regrets
to hang about your neck
to strangle your hopes,
dreams,
aspirations.
Doubt, Jealousies
like harpies,
Ugly, Ugly thoughts;
there is always something of them
lurking in
the shadow cast by bright light
hungering to devour all but their dark.
Beware!

    I stumble.
I stutter.
I lash out, hurling my arms, waving my fists
at emptiness.
"What do you want of me?"
"Step aside.
Let Liet go.
The path of the Fey-fi is not your path.
You are crow,
one that follows."
"We all follow.
Whether I follow Liet or some other path, is my choice."

"Oh, listen to it now
adopting the philosophy.
'My path is my choice.' That may be.
But first you must find this path.
And then —
how is choosing done?
Of all the paths that offer themselves,
of all the ways to get there from here,
how does one determine which is theirs?
Do you know, Crow?
Can you show us?
Can you, for instance,
find the path between the north and west?
Follow that path,
join Liet there,
and you are free to take up the Feya-fi.
Agree to this and you have your chance."
"Then, yes, I agree. I must."

　　　Where do I go from here?
To get from here to there,
to find the path between the north and west,
requires an inner vision.
I must see it with my own eyes.
If it is meant to be,
the path will be open to me
and I will know which way to go.
There is no use in a map.
I can ask no one directions.
There is no description,
oral or written,
capable of capturing the path to be chosen.

It must be clear before me.
To envision the Feya-fi,
to get from here to there is done only in the going.
So I go.

    I set out
without Scout or any of the others.
I head for a point familiar and near where I am
    to join Liet.
Sudden follows.
I have not asked her to come
but she stays with me.
Fido.

    From there we walk as many paths as possible.
I wear them out, wear them right out,
work them for any and all sign available.
Sudden and I walk the path,
walk it,
walk it,
walk,
lose our way,
backtrack,
chase our tails
well into the night,
night after night.
Our bright "Yes!" of beginnings
gives way to days dark
and all gray.
The sun barely makes a show.
Our daily struggle rises in the east void of highlights
and even the riddle of induction cannot offer escape.

I dream of betrayals.
There are snakes in the road
and each morning I awake
more and more confused.
Brightness is dimming.

So, when
is the moment hope surrenders?
And the future slips away from (our) plans and dreams?
And (our) hearts do not want to want
and yet go on beating?

I see that I have come to my end.
The path is gone before me
and I am
abandoned.

Come the final evening
I am on the bluff
above whitewater.
My unraveled plans
cascade down the rock face,
plummet into the river
and take off from me too quickly.
On the opposite bank sits Liet,
an invisible enchanted presence,
like one's happy childhood.
Between us, the great chasm ever-widening up,
all the way up
to the sky
swallowing whole
the magic of our time together,

the length of its days,
the breadth of its beauty,
entire alphabets.
The sun sets.
We watch over one another
and write in the water's foam and roar below
all our power
to hold on forever.
We let it go
down stream to meet the ocean broken;
a piece of you,
a piece of me.

I read on
in the water over rocks,
the smell of wet earth,
the seam between the land and the river
of friendship, of longing, of what might have been
written in Liet's hand.
When I am done,
it is hours since Liet has left the embankment and gone
on
into the trees and woods that border the Great Path
that now is home
to a new freed soul.
Alphabets are fading.
All around me they withdraw with the sun.

Before I go blind to all this deep mystery,
I am given a vision of the Feya-fi
in the distance
out of reach of me.
The golden gleaming leading
all the way to the horizon
and beyond,
humming like the speed of light,
calling,
calls
to me
"Someday."

epilogue

✳
•

I come to you,
I bring this story,
and all the while, there are black crows
waiting
in the road.
They are gathering.
Let them gather.
Let them come.
I am done and ready to follow them again.
Though no path holds such magic as those
    walked with the genG,
between us we manage some
of the sparkle
that fades in the wake of the mudpeople.
I have my vision of the Feya-fi;
I have my memory
of the play between day and night.
I carry these
up the hill

slowly,
open them and my very self to the landscape,
listen,
listen with all my skill and devotion.
But my fluency ebbs and flows
tidally.
I only see it written everywhere
"We are never lost to those who long for our return."
I dedicate my life to these,
I dedicate this story,
to the one who always waits for me
(yes, you, Dan),
to those I loved like my brother
in whose sorrow this was born;
to those who perished on September 11th
while I wrote on.
Forgive me.
Doesn't Destruction demand justice from us?
Doesn't It demand Affirmation?
I give it with both hands open.
I give it when I lay among the evergreens
and mouth the words into the dark
silently:
"To stand under a yellow tree, imagining."
And then
somewhere the story begins.